THE
SHAPE GAME

From June 2001 until March 2002 I worked as the writer and illustrator in residence at Tate Britain in London. This was part of a 3-year project called Visual Paths, developed by the Tate in partnership with the Institute of Education. I worked with a thousand children from inner-city schools, teaching literacy using the resources within the gallery. My intention was to create a new book based on responses to works of art in the Tate collections, and to conduct workshops with the children and their teachers. I remember it as a time that changed my life forever...

I must thank Colin Grigg, Co-ordinator of Visual Paths who was as inspirational as the paintings, and the children of these schools who played the shape game so wonderfully (as all children do):

Churchill Gardens Primary School
Gloucester Primary School
Henry Fawcett Primary School
Latham Primary School
Marianne Richardson Primary School
Michael Faraday Primary School
Saint Gabriel's Primary School
Saint Mark's Primary School
Shapla Primary School
Vicarage Primary School
Langdon School

For my brother Michael, who spent hours playing the shape game with me. A.B.

THE SHAPE GAME
A PICTURE CORGI BOOK 978 0 552 54696 6

Published in Great Britain by Picture Corgi Books,
an imprint of Random House Children's Publishers UK

Doubleday edition published 2003
Picture Corgi edition published 2004

10

Picture Corgi Books are published by Random House Children's Publishers UK,
61–63 Uxbridge Road, London W5 5SA,
A RANDOM HOUSE GROUP COMPANY
Addresses for companies within The Random House Group Limited
can be found at : www.randomhouse.co.uk/offices.htm

THE RANDOM HOUSE GROUP Limited Reg. No. 954009
www.randomhousechildrens.co.uk

A CIP catalogue record for this book is available from the British Library.

Printed in Singapore

THE
SHAPE GAME

Anthony Browne

Picture Corgi

I was a little boy and didn't know what to expect.
It was my mother's idea — that year for her birthday
she wanted us all to go somewhere different.
It turned out to be a day that changed my life forever.

Dad

Mum

George

me

We went on a train to the city and then had a long walk.
There was an important match on the telly so I knew
Dad and George didn't really want to come. George spent most of
the time trying to trip me up, and Dad told us some of his jokes.
"Why do gorillas have huge nostrils?"

"I don't know," said George.

"Because they've got huge fingers!" said Dad.

All his jokes were like that.

When we got there the place looked really posh.

I felt a bit nervous and even George and Dad were quiet.
(At first.)

"What on earth is that supposed to be?" asked Dad.
"It's supposed to be a mother and child," said Mum.
"Well, why isn't it?" said Dad.

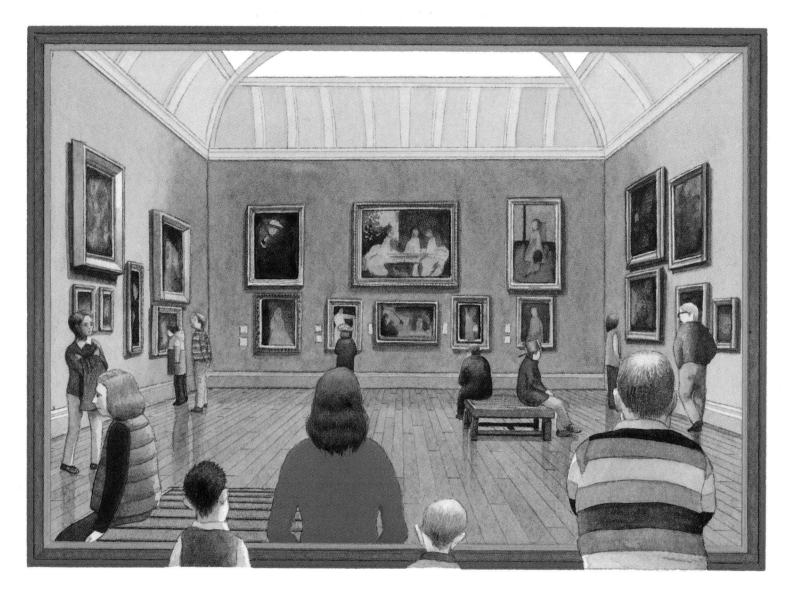

Mum took us into a large room that was full of old paintings.
"Boring," said George, and Dad told him to shut up.
(I thought it looked boring too, but I wasn't sure.)

George leaned against a picture
and one of the guards came and told him off.
So Dad told him off too.
It wasn't a very good start to the visit, especially for George.

John Martin: The Great Day of His Wrath

Dad tried to cheer him up: "Did you hear about the
fool who keeps going round saying no?"

"No," George mumbled.

"Oh, so it's you then!" Dad said, laughing.

George wandered away.

Augustus Egg, *Past and Present No.1*

Mum talked to us about a painting of a family. "Does it remind you of a family we know?" asked Mum, but she was smiling.
She said that the father was holding a love letter written to his wife by another man, and that there were lots of clues in the picture that told us more of the story. So we all worked it out:

Adam and Eve were thrown out of Paradise after Eve was tempted to eat the serpent's apple. The Mother also was tempted – by the other man.

In the mirror we can see an open door showing that the mother will have to leave home.

Portrait of the mother.

The broken ship is abandoned by its crew, and the man also feels abandoned by his wife.

Portrait of the father.

The children's house of cards is falling down, like their happy family life.

Portrait of the other man.

The bad half of the apple, like the woman, has fallen on the floor.

The woman has fallen to the floor because she's so upset, and the bracelets on her wrists are painted to look like handcuffs.

"It's gone, gone forever, I tell you!" said Dad.
"What has?" I asked.
"Yesterday!" said Dad.

British School seventeenth century: The Cholmondeley Ladies

"Those two are just the same," I said.

"Well, not exactly," said Mum. "Look more closely."

SPOT THE DIFFERENCE

These pictures are not the same – how many differences can you see?

John Singleton Copley: *The Death of Major Peirson*

In the next room George called, "Hey, look at this – it's GREAT!"

"Do you think so?" said Mum.
"Can you imagine that really happening in our street?"

Sir John Everett Millais: *The Boyhood of Raleigh*

"Does that remind you of anything?" asked Mum.

"It reminds me of Dad telling us one of his jokes," I said.

George Stubbs: *Horse Devoured by a Lion*

"Now that's what I call a painting," said Dad.
"Look at that lion – it's SO REAL!"

And it was.

"Did you hear about the little boy they named after his father?" asked Dad.

"No," I said.

"They called him Dad!" said Dad.

There was a loud silence, but we all started laughing when we saw a painting of a man who looked a bit like Dad.

It was time to go, and on the way out we called in
at the gift shop. All we bought were these.

We walked back to get the train and everyone was in a good mood.
When we got to the station Dad asked,
"What did Batman say to Robin before they got in the car?"

"Oh all right then," said Mum. "What _did_ Batman say to
Robin before he got in the car?"

"Robin, get in the car!" replied Dad.

"Come on boys," said Mum. "Get in the train."

On the way home Mum showed us a brilliant drawing game
that she used to play with her dad. The first person draws a
shape – any shape, it's not supposed to be anything, just a shape.

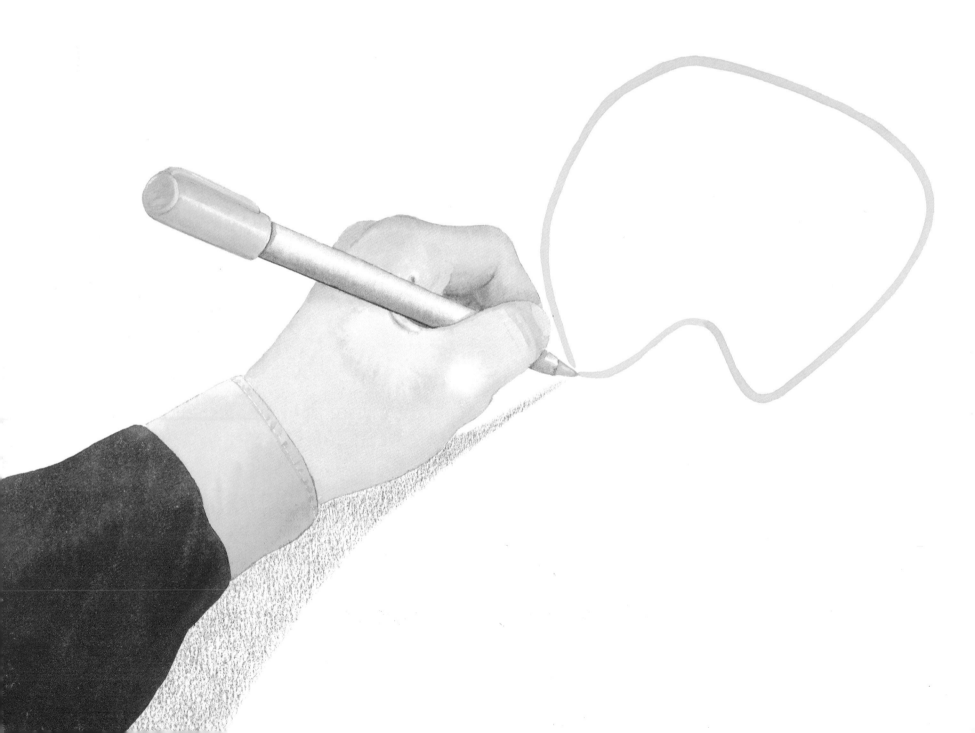

The next person has to change it into something.
It's fantastic, we all played it for the rest of the journey.

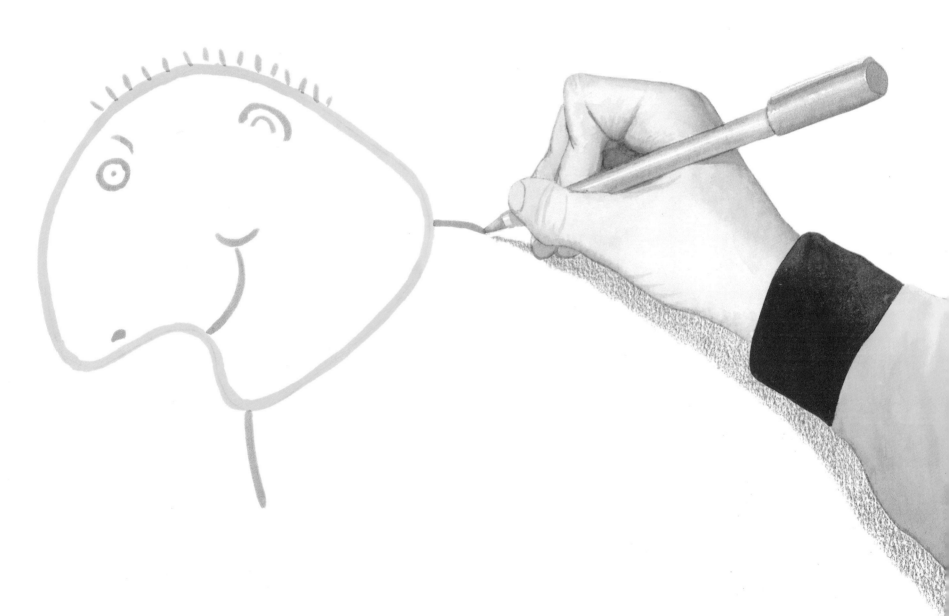

And, in a way, I've been playing the shape game ever since...